Snowed In With My Best Friend

Copyright

First Edition, February 2025

Paperback ISBN: 978-1-961966-77-2

Published by: Carxander Publishing
Wisconsin

Dedication

To all the girlies who have that hot, dominant best friend you're head over heels in love with but believe you'll never get the chance to try and be more…

Opening Quote

I empty the bottle and empty my soul. I sleep with the devil, and I wake up alone. I'm kicking myself while I pick up my clothes. I make the same mistakes, and I pray all the way home.

Pray All The Way Home by Austin Snell

Chapter One

❄ Emma ❄

I scratch my nails down Jake's back as I arch into him. "Oh, holy... yes...," I moan as I meet him thrust for thrust. Our hips smack against each other's. I'm so wet, the noises it makes are nothing less than filthy.

"My tight little princess likes being fucked rough," Jake rumbles.

This is wrong. He's my best friend. We're going to ruin the relationship. I know it. This is so wrong...

...but it feels so, so right.

I wrap my legs around him tighter. He slides in deeper as he pounds into me.

Harder.

Harder.

"Jake!" I scream as he brings me higher and higher. My pussy tightens around him as his cock gets impossibly thicker. "Oh, Jake!" I keep meeting his thrusts.

"You're gonna come for me. Right now. You're gonna show me how much you love my dick fucking you."

"Ah! Jake!" I scream as my entire body explodes into a firework, obeying his command like he's a drill sergeant.

"Em!" Jake shouts as he stiffens. He slams his dick deep inside me one more time and comes with a roar. "Fuck!"

My body jerks into him as he fills me. I'm trembling. I can barely hold onto him, but I'm trying my best. Finally, he collapses on me and rolls us both over to our sides as his cock slides out of me. His come, intermingled with mine, makes a mess of my thighs and the sheets beneath us.

I cuddle into him as we both catch our breath.

Oh my... I just had the best sex I've ever had with my best friend.

The gravity of the situation hits me like a 747 jet plane.

No.

This can't have happened. We're never going to be the same after this. Friendships don't survive this kind of intimacy. And while I want more, he never has. I can't be in a friends with benefits situation, so one thing is very clear to me...

I just lost my best friend...

❄❄❄

Honk!

I jump and glance in my rearview mirror before I start driving again. I zoned out at the four-way stop. How embarrassing. I give a little wave of apology as I glance at my GPS.

After Jake fell asleep last night, I quickly got my stuff and left him in his bed. I hurried home and grabbed some things. I needed to get away. So, I threw a dart at the map I have pinned to the wall in my bedroom. I'm a big fan of geography. I don't work in the field, but I should. I often get obsessed with it. Especially volcanoes and volcanic activity. I should've become a volcanologist.

The dart landed on Rexford, Colorado. I'm from Cody, Wyoming. It's an eight hour drive from Cody to Rexford, but I don't mind it. The scenery is gorgeous, and I have time to clear my head.

And get Jake Blackwood out of it.

Why does Jake have to be so insanely good looking? He's six feet five, built like a god, carved from marble. His eyes are so green that a person looking into them could melt. He's got this half smirk that makes panties fly off women the second he flashes it. I should know…

I've been in love with Jake ever since we met when his family moved to Cody. He was in eighth grade. I was in sixth. We became fast friends the day I was hurrying to class and nearly ran him over. Everyone was laughing at me as my books flew all over the place, but the moment our bodies collided, I knew he was the one.

If people knew that, they'd call me crazy, but the heart and body know what they want. It doesn't matter when it happens. And from that day forward, Jake and I were inseparable. We lived next door to each other. His dad worked on my family's ranch. He still does. My dad liked them as much as me and moved them into the cottage we had next to our house. When he went to high school, he still walked with me to my school. When I got to high school, we hung out all of the time together, even though he was two years ahead of me. I went to all of his football games.

We made everyone jealous because everyone wanted a piece of the city's star quarterback. Every girlfriend he had hated me, but he always told them that I'm like his little sister. We're a package deal. His relationships never lasted long.

Honestly, they still don't. He was with one girl that I actually got along with really well. They dated for three years before he broke up with her. She was cheating on him the whole time they were together. I hated not seeing it because I was around her so much. I never knew. Jake was in the Army and deployed overseas during much of their relationship. I should've kept a better eye on things. He was so heartbroken.

But through all the years, all seventeen of them, we've both been the constant in each other's lives. We've been there for each other when times were tough. We celebrated each other's wins. Cried with each other during losses.

I sigh.

And I fell in love with him.

I pull into the parking lot of the adorable bed and breakfast I found when I stopped for gas. I was lucky when I called to see if they had rooms available. They only had one, and it's the honeymoon suite. I looked at pictures of it and was impressed with the hot tub, fireplace, large bed, sitting area, and the incredible floor to ceiling windows with a beautiful view of a small lake and gorgeous wooded area. I was so happy they had a room available. And even more happy it was available for two weeks. I paid right away.

I get out of my car and hug myself against the chill. There's a lot of snow on the ground, and it's starting to fall a little. I'm used to the cold but this windchill is nothing to play with.

I hurry inside the cabin-like bed and breakfast after grabbing my stuff. Once I get inside, I'm happy to feel how warm and toasty it is. The entire lobby is decorated in adorable Valentine's Day decor. I make my way to the front desk and look around for whoever is supposed to be checking people in. I see a couple of people near a fireplace in what looks like a cute little library, but they're drinking something hot and reading. I don't think it's the people who own this place.

I sniff when a delicious smell hits my nose. "Oh my… Is that…?" Biscuits and gravy. That's what it is. I'd know that smell anywhere. It's my all time favorite food. Sausage gravy… flaky biscuits… Mmm… There's nothing better.

I let my nose lead me to the kitchen and see a slender woman with short, gray, wavy hair bending over the oven and taking something out while the gravy I knew I smelled simmers on a burner. She puts the biscuits on a cutting board, and I choose that moment to quietly clear my throat.

She turns quickly and smiles. She's an older woman who looks just as friendly in person as she sounded on the phone. Her soft smile is big, and her gray eyes are lit up. I can't help but smile just as genuinely back at her.

"Oh, dear, I'm so sorry I didn't hear you come in!" she exclaims as she hurries towards me. "Look at you! You must be freezing."

"I'm okay, ma'am. Really."

"No 'ma'am' out of you. It makes me feel old." She laughs. "Mavis Danvers is the name. And you're Emma Marsden."

I nod. "That's me!"

"Let's get you sat down for dinner. We'll check you in after."

"I'll check her in, Mave," a deep voice says behind me. I turn to see a tall man with a little bit of facial hair and salt and pepper hair. "Hi,

I'm Ronny Danvers. Mavis' husband. We'll let her finish up in here and get you all checked in just in time for dinner."

"Perfect."

I follow Mr. Danvers out to the desk. He has me quickly checked in and hands me my keys. I see Mrs. Danvers putting out dinner as lots of hungry guests start trailing into the dining room. The table is large enough to fit a lot of people. It feels so much like a family, and I really love that added touch.

Instead of going straight to my room, I decide to eat dinner first. It's just as delicious as it smells and definitely filling. The people staying here are all very sweet and friendly. As I make my way to my room finally, I know I made the right choice in coming.

After letting myself in and admiring everything the room has to offer, including the giant tub in the bathroom and four-post, King-sized bed next to a floor to ceiling window with a glass door leading out to a balcony, I yawn. I'm truly exhausted, but I can't stop looking at the cabin-like room, complete with wooden walls, dressers, and stands. The bedframe is even wood. It smells like cedar, and I'm already in love. I never want to leave.

I yawn again and decide I'll put my things away in the morning. I'm just about to crawl into bed after getting ready when someone knocks on my door. I jump and look for something to cover up with. I'm only wearing a pair of skimpy shorts and an even skimpier tank top.

Unable to find anything quickly, and anxious about opening the door to see who's on the other side after the second, more urgent knock, I hurry without covering myself. What if there's a fire and they're warning me to get out? I don't want to keep them waiting if it's an emergency.

I open the door after unlocking it and nearly choke.

I have to be dreaming. There's no way I'm face to face with the object of all of my fantasies and the man I ran from.

Jake fucking Blackwood…

"Well, you gonna invite me in?" he asks, his voice, smooth as silk, sending vibrations through my whole body that settle between my legs.

I can't speak. Instead, I stare into his deep green eyes like if I look away, I'll drown…

Chapter Two

❄ Jake ❄

"Are you going to invite me in?" I ask after I catch my breath. Emma Marsden is the most beautiful woman I've ever met. Ever since we met when we were kids, I've thought that.

Neither of us made a move, though. And that was something I'm going to regret for the rest of my life. I lost so much time with her. An entire lifetime already. We might have always been by each other's side supporting each other, but not the way I wanted us to be.

It never felt like it was something she wanted. We came from different worlds. We lived right next to each other, but she was in the library while I was on gridiron. At my games, she was always cheering me on, but it was from behind everyone else. I always knew where she was sitting, though. I always picked her out among the crowd every time.

She was never interested in me, though. At least I didn't think so. I was too wrapped up in being a fucking teenager and stupid Army kid. I made a lot of mistakes. I never should've been in any other relationship. Never should've been with other women. Never should have had all those one-night stands and slept around. It's always been Emma. She's always been the one for me. I was just too stupid to see it; to push it.

Until last night.

Last night was the best night of my life. We were both completely sober and knew exactly what we were doing. I kissed her after a buddy's birthday party. She looked way too good. She showed up alone, and so did I. Like we usually do, we paired up for all the dancing and shit because everyone else in our friend group has a significant other. We've paired up before. It's never bothered us.

Something about last night, though… The way she looked in that sexy black dress. The pretty red heels that matched the lingerie underneath that I wasn't supposed to see but did when she tried to carefully kneel to get her wallet when she dropped it. I went into instant protective mode. I pulled her up immediately and got her wallet myself. Her dress was way too short, and I didn't want anyone else to see her but me.

"How did you get here?" Emma whispers.

Her sweet, almost broken voice cuts through my thoughts. "You have GPS on your phone… Remember?"

She furrows her pretty eyebrows. "You… tracked me?" She crosses her arms over her chest, pushing up her ample tits. It doesn't help the hard on I already have after seeing her in that skimpy sleepwear. Her long, golden brown hair falls over her shoulders. I can see the hardened peaks of her nipples through the thin, satin material of her tank top. The shorts show off the perfect heart shape of her ass. An ass I was gripping not even twenty-four hours ago.

"What did you expect me to do, Em? You disappeared. Not only from my bed, but your own apartment. I didn't really even have to track you. You left the dart in your wish map."

Her eyes widen at me calling it her wish map. She'll tell everyone it's because she loves maps, but I know her. That map is up because, sometimes, she likes to just take off on a trip to anywhere because she can. She used to do it all the time when I was deployed. She said it was because she was bored without me. I knew she was telling the truth, but I also hated that she went on those trips alone. A beautiful girl in Rome or Paris is easy to take advantage of. She told me she was going to Mexico once, and I forbade her from doing it without me.

She listened to me because she always does, and I've never been more grateful for it.

"So? Are you letting me in?"

Emma sighs and steps aside. I walk in, my duffel bag swung over my shoulder. I take in the room and whistle between my teeth. "Damn nice room you got."

"It was all they had left." Her eyes widen just as I turn. "Jake, you… we…" Her eyes dart to the bed then back to me. "There's only one bed! You can't stay here! And they're booked!"

I raise an eyebrow and slowly put my duffel bag down. "This is a problem, how?"

"We… just…" She's fucking adorable when she's flustered. I can't help but grin as I watch her flutter around the room. "We can't! We… Oh my god, Jake." She stops and looks up at me. Emma is only five feet. I tower over her, and I love it. She's a small woman, and I'm definitely not a small man. We fit together perfectly.

Though I'm thoroughly enjoying watching her so out of sorts, I decide to put her out of her misery. I take her hand and lead her to the bed. "Em, come on. We have to talk about this."

"We could forget about it."

I shake my head, a little taken aback as I sit down, pulling her next to me. "What?"

"I just… don't want to ruin anything." She looks down at her pretty feet with the pink, painted toenails.

I start to say something, but I suddenly understand and close my mouth, choosing my next words carefully. After a few moments, I take both of her hands in mine and turn towards her. What I'm about to say is going to cut me deep, but I know her well. She's terrified that if things escalate between us, she'll become another notch in my bedpost. I know I'm not considered the one who got away for anyone, but damn, she'll be mine.

I really wanted to be her forever.

I know better, though. Emma is way too good for a man like me. She deserves everything I could never give her. Her parents own a giant ranch in Wyoming. It's very well off, and her family is extremely well to do. They're one of the most prominent families in Cody. Fuck. All of Wyoming.

My dad is a ranch hand for them. He's more than that now. He's like the second in command if anyone needs anything. Me and Emma hit it off so fast when my dad first got the job that we moved into a cottage next to their house on their property. My parents still live there. Our families are still very close.

I hope they'll stay that way after this.

I take a deep breath. "Listen, Em. Yesterday was a mistake." My chest feels like it's on fire as bile rises from my stomach at the lie. I don't think it was a mistake at all, but I'm always gonna give her what she needs. "I don't want to ruin anything either. So, let's just forget it happened and move on, okay? We've been friends for so long. This is just a bump in the road."

She lets out a visible sigh of relief as she looks up at me. Her tiny hands squeeze mine. "Really? You promise that it didn't ruin anything? Because I just… I don't want to ever not be without you in my life."

It pains me, but I give her a tight nod as I force a smile. "Yeah. I promise. I obviously want you in my life." *Any way you'll have me.* I don't say those words out loud, but I want to.

She smiles. Her pretty golden eyes light up and make my pulse quicken. Suddenly, she's back to being the girl I know. Fun loving and carefree. "Thank you, Jake. I really thought you were going to hate me."

"In what world is that an even remote possibility?" I bury my face in her hair and close my eyes. The smell of coconut calms my tumultuous emotions. This isn't what I want. What I want is her.

"I think we should watch movies."

"I'm down for that." *I'll do anything you want if it means you don't run away again.*

I make my way to the bathroom with my duffel bag to clean up as Emma gets ready to watch movies. After closing the door, I turn and take a deep breath as I grip the bathroom counter. I close my eyes, willing myself to calm the fuck down. It's not about me. It's never been about me. It's always been about her and always will be. She's the one who keeps my demons from consuming me. I saw a lot when I was overseas. She keeps those images nicely tucked away.

I really want more with her. I was a fucking fool to think she did, too. There's no place for me in this world without her. If that means I don't get her any other way than this, I'll take it.

I'm nothing without her. She kills the pain, and that's more than worth the price of the heartbreak I'm feeling right now.

I need her to keep the reaper off my back…

…even though she's slowly killing me…

Chapter Three

❄ Emma ❄

"Mmm…," I mumble with a yawn as I blink my eyes open. I lay still for a few moments as I orient myself to my surroundings.

It takes me a few minutes, but I slowly start to realize I'm not alone in this way too comfortable bed. Like a tidal wave, everything that happened the past couple of days comes back to me. The best sex of my life with Jake, my best friend, all the way to him showing up in Rexford after I ran away, and to us falling asleep next to each other. Just like so many times before.

Only this time, I'm acutely aware of the hard on against my lower back. I've felt it before, but it's different this time. This time it makes me want to turn around in his arms, pull down his gray sweats that show off his length way too well, and start sucking him off. I'm obsessed with how he tastes.

Oh god. No, I can't be like this with him. It'll ruin everything we've built. I'll lose him. I try to get up, but he pulls me closer, his arms locking around me. It forces me to try and squiggle away from him.

"Em, stop moving," Jake says, his voice sexy as hell. It's raspy and filled with sleep.

"I have to… g-go to the bathroom."

"Fuck…" He slowly lets me go with a low sigh that has me shivering. He did that when his mouth was against my pussy, and he almost made me come right then and there.

I leap out of the bed when he lets me go. I can't think of that. I can't think of how many times he made me come. Or how good it feels to wake up with his hard dick against me. Or how good it feels to be in his arms.

Safe.

I hurry to the bathroom and close myself in. I take my time going through my morning routine, including an extra long shower. It doesn't help to get the images of Jake out of my head, though. I can't stop thinking about him. The way his muscles move when I'm riding him. The way he grips my hips when he wants to pound into me.

It doesn't matter how many times I try to make the images stop, I can still see them. I feel everything. Every ridge, thrust, touch…

Before I know what I'm doing, my hand is between my thighs to relieve the pressure. My stomach is tight, and I'm already tingling just thinking of him naked. I'll never see it again, but at least I saw it and can use it to fantasize.

I lean against the shower wall and close my eyes. The water cascades over my body. With one hand, I start rubbing my nipples and pinching them as I play with my clit. I slide my middle finger inside myself and think of how good it felt when Jake did it.

"Oh god… Jake…," I whisper.

Just his name on my lips sends me over the edge. I clench tight around my finger and keep rubbing my clit. I squeeze my own tits and let out a quiet gasp, whispering his name once more as my release washes over me like the spray from the shower. I tremble and pant as I rub my clit through my orgasm and squeeze my thighs shut.

I jump when I hear a knock on the door. "Em? You gonna be much longer? Hate to rush you, but I'm gonna end up pissing off the balcony if you don't hurry up."

My eyes widen. I hurry to finish my shower. "I'm sorry! I didn't mean to take so long!" I shut the water off.

"I deserved it," he rumbles. I'm pretty sure I wasn't meant to hear it.

I bite my lip wondering what he meant, or if I even heard him right. Maybe he didn't say that, and I just thought he did. Maybe I'm making too much of a deal out of this. Maybe I'm stupid for pushing him away.

I know I am. I shake my head. I really am. I'm just so scared that things are going to be ruined. Friendships never last when something like this happens, and I don't want to lose him. I love him so much, my heart aches at the thought of him not being around me. He's so great. Way out of my league and too good for me. My relationships never last. I'm always told I'm toxic and a horrible girlfriend. He deserves better than that.

I shake myself out of my self-loathing and hurry to dry off. I wrap a towel around myself and wrap my hair in one. I take my brush and lotion with me so he can do what he needs to do. When I open the door, he's leaning against the wall. His sweats hang low on his hips. Low enough to show off the V that leads to his nine inch, perfectly thick dick.

I quickly look away. "I'm sorry. I didn't mean to take that long."

He pushes off the wall and heads into the bathroom without saying anything. I sigh when he closes the door. Things really feel different with us. I don't like it. I want things to be the same as they always have been.

I don't realize how much time has gone by until I'm dressed and have finished putting all of my stuff away after brushing my hair. I look at the clock on the nightstand and see it's been an hour. I don't hear the shower running anymore. I tilt my head and walk towards the bathroom slowly, listening. I nibble my lower lip. I do that when I'm nervous. It's a habit I'm trying to break. I'm just about to knock on the door when I hear him grunting.

"Fuck…," he moans breathily.

I put a hand over my mouth because I know exactly what he's doing. I hurry away from it and sit on the bed. I grab my phone and start scrolling through reels on Instagram. Anything to make it look like I didn't hear anything he was doing.

"Did he hear me when I did it?" I ask myself barely above a whisper.

"Did I hear you what, Em?"

I jump and drop my phone as my eyes snap to him. He's got nothing but a towel wrapped around his waist. His hair is damp. His abs are just as tight as they were the other night when I was licking them.

Stop it! I command myself. *He's off limits in all of the ways!*

"Nothing," I say in a voice too high to sound normal. He raises an eyebrow and smirks but says nothing. Instead, he looks for his duffel bag. "Oh, um. I put your stuff away already. I hope that's okay."

He nods and walks towards the dresser. "Em, you always do that whenever we disappear like this. Why would I mind?"

I smile softly. I love when he goes on these little trips with me. He doesn't know it, and never will, but I pretend we're a couple when we go together. It's a dumb fantasy, but it helps keep me calm and out of my head.

I clear my throat. "Um. We slept in… I thought maybe we could go out to lunch and maybe go shopping for a few things. I looked at the weather, and it looks like there's a storm coming. Maybe we could get snacks and stuff?"

"Yeah. Whatever you want. Lunch sounds good. The town looks like fun, too."

I smile brightly, feeling a little more normal when he turns and smiles at me. He heads to the bathroom to get dressed, and my heart lightens a little.

Once he finishes, we head to town in his Dodge Charger. We find a nice place for lunch before we take time to walk around the main part of the town. We stop in shops, and I find cute things I can take home with me to remind me of the town. I have an entire room in my apartment with a collection of things from all of the places I've been.

"Thank you," Jake says as the adorable young girl hands him a couple bags filled with all of our snacks.

"You're welcome. Enjoy!" she says. She's blond and cute. She can't be any older than sixteen and is very peppy and cheerful. She has the kind of smile that people can't help but smile back at. "You guys are such an adorable couple!"

Jake grins. "Thanks, but just friends."

I give her a soft smile as we both turn away. She's blushing, and I can't help the pang of jealousy in the pit of my stomach. Jake didn't do anything but speak the truth, but I hate the way she looked at him after she found out we weren't together. I know he'd never go after someone her age, but I still hate how I feel right now.

I don't have the right to be jealous. I wanted this. I wanted for us to just be friends. I have no reason to be jealous of anyone and shouldn't be upset when he corrects people and says we're friends.

It's just that he never has. He's never made it a point to do that. Maybe that's why it hurts so much. It's one more thing that feels different in our relationship now, and that scares me.

I hurry out of the general store into the cold, bitter air before I start crying. This was a mistake. Everything was a mistake. Maybe I really am toxic. I never understood how. Maybe this is how. Jealous for no reason.

"Emma, what's wrong?" Jake asks, his deep voice etched with concern as he reaches for my hand. I pull it away. Pain crosses his handsome face, and it breaks me even more. Everyone I've ever dated is right about me. I'm a horrible person.

I shake my head. "It's changed, Jake," I whisper. "And it's my fault. I fucked up."

His eyebrows shoot up in concern. Probably because I rarely swear. "What are you talking about? What's going on?" He reaches for my hand again, but I take a couple steps backwards and hug myself. More pain flashes in his eyes.

"You never correct anyone when they say stuff about us being a couple," I tell him. My chest physically hurts. I feel like I'm having a heart attack. My head feels like it might explode. It's tingling, and I'm dizzy. But I fight it, I fight it all because I don't want him to see me collapse into a crying mess. "You should just go back to Cody before the storm hits."

"Em, come on. I didn't -"

"Don't. Just don't, Jake. Just go." I take the bags and hurry away. I shake my head in frustration at myself and how stupid I am. I should've told him that I wanted to be with him. Fuck not wanting to ruin our friendship. I just want him.

But it's too late.

"Fuck, come on. Don't be like this," Jake says, his voice cracking.

I don't turn around, as painful as it is. I keep walking. The B&B isn't that far away. It will only take me fifteen minutes to walk it.

I'm so lost in my head that I don't notice I've somehow gotten turned around. It's dark, and I don't know where I am.

I turn when I see lights, hoping against all hope that it's Jake.

But it's not. It's a truck, and the driver is slowing down. He pulls up beside me as the window comes down. "You look a little lost," he drawls, chewing on a toothpick. He's got a dark beard and shaved head. I don't know how tall he is, but he looks like he could be a lumberjack. "Help you, little lady?"

I shake my head nervously. "N-no thanks," I say as firmly as I can while taking my phone out of my jacket pocket. "I-I just got a little t-turned around." I'm stuttering. I hate doing that. It shows fear. Jake always told me to never show fear.

"Oh, come on, now. Don't be stubborn. Where ya headed?"

I look up directions to the B&B and nearly cry when I see my battery is low. Jake has called me and texted multiple times, but I don't have enough battery to call him. Before my phone shuts off, I quickly see that I made a wrong turn and have to go back. *I'm so dumb. How could I forget to charge my phone? I wish I could call Jake. I hope he hasn't left yet.*

"I just got turned around," I say, taking a deep breath and smiling as I turn around. "Thank you for stopping, but I'm really okay." I start walking back the way I came.

"Don't be like that, now, girl! I'll happily take you wherever you need to go!"

"I'm okay!" I quicken my pace and breathe a sigh of relief as he starts driving slowly away.

Unfortunately, I'm not that lucky. My grip tightens on the handles of the bags I'm carrying as the guy turns around. *Oh God, please, please make him go away.*

I don't know why I bother praying to a god who has never done a thing for me, but I'm scared and it's my only option. Especially since the temp is dropping. If I have to run through the woods, I'd freeze to death if the guy didn't catch me and kill me first.

"Don't be difficult, little lady. You'll catch your death out here. The air temp is below zero."

"I'm really okay. Thank you!" I keep trying to be polite, but I quicken my pace. I don't like that this person isn't taking no for an answer. He could be the nicest person in the world, but he's giving off creepy vibes.

“Don’t be a little bitch. Get in the truck.” His voice drops an octave, and I shiver. Definitely not a nice guy.

I say nothing. I walk faster and keep my eyes ahead. I see another set of headlights and hope that whoever it is will see something’s wrong and help me. When they fly by, not even slowing down, I start crying.

I never should’ve left Jake in town and decided to walk back to the B&B. I’m going to die out here, and he’s never gonna know I really feel about him.

Chapter Four

❄ Jake ❄

"Emma. It's Jake again. I'm really worried. I didn't see you on the way to the B&B. You're not in the room. No one here has seen you. I know you're pissed at me, but pick up. Please." I sigh and hang up the phone again.

I'm not doing any good here. I grab my coat and keys and walk out of our room. I'm confused. I don't know what happened, exactly, but I know she's angry and hurt. I don't like that. I need to fix it. I realize where we both went wrong, and now I need to make it right.

Fuck, I never should've let her walk away. It took me talking to an old friend to realize she's never going to be just a friend. She's always been more than that. I want her in my life. I want to spend the rest of my life with her. I might not make it out alive, but I'm going to love her for the rest of my life.

"Did you find her, Mr. Blackwood?" Mrs. Danvers asks me, her worry lines very evident as she nibbles her lip.

I shake my head. "Not yet, but I'm going to." I look down at my phone and quickly pull up her phone so I can pin her location. I don't know why I didn't think of this thirty fucking minutes ago. I head for the door as soon as it pins her. She's not far, but I stop in my tracks when her location disappears. "Fuck," I whisper. I turn back to Mrs. Danvers. "Where's this?" I point to the spot on my phone where it showed her.

"That's just down the road like you're going to town. Turn right at the stop sign onto Owl Way."

I nod again and squeeze her arm lightly before almost running to my car. It's snowing now and starting to come down heavily. That storm they said is coming is definitely here. I need to find her quick.

I pull out of my parking spot as I turn on my lights and windshield wipers. I put on my seatbelt when I hit the road. I know going as fast as I want to is out of the question, but it doesn't mean I don't push it. I want to get to her safely but fast.

I start slowing down well before the stop sign. After seeing it's all clear, I make my turn onto Owl Way. This was the road she was on. I'm hoping she didn't veer off somewhere. I slow down even more so I don't miss her. The snow is getting heavier, and she's a small woman. She's also wearing a white coat and white boots.

"Fuck, I'm getting her a different color coat and boots immediately." Yeah. Immediately after I fuck this disobedience out of her. Why the hell would she just run from me? Twice. We've always been able to talk shit out.

Keeping my eyes on the side of the road as I creep along, I growl at myself. She ran because I gave into her fear and told her we could be just friends. I know her better than that. I've spent years getting to know everything about her. Never should've given into her fear.

One of the biggest things I've learned about her is her voice gets quiet when she's keeping something from me or not telling me the truth. Her voice did that this morning when we were talking. I didn't pay attention to her. I was too busy in my own head. This entire thing is solely my fault.

I pull over and hit my brakes when I catch a glimpse of someone running. At least that's what I think it is. It could be a wolf, for all I know. I jump out of the car after throwing it in park.

"Help me!" a voice I would know anywhere screams.

I start running towards her. "Em!" I call out so she knows it's me.

"Jake! Help me!" Emma screams even louder. Like a missile, she leaps into my arms.

But my eyes are on the man barreling at me from behind her.

Quickly, I push Emma towards the car. "Get in the car, Em. Now."

Thankfully, she doesn't argue. She runs to the car. I ball my fists, ready for a fight. I can't see the guy clearly yet, but I can make out the flannel and the headlights of a parked truck not far away. I can see the guy stop and run in the opposite direction. I have half a mind to chase him, but I push that part way down. There's too many things that could happen, so I turn and dart back to the car.

Once I'm in, I want to pull Emma into my arms and comfort her, but I can't. I have to get us to safety. I don't dare turn around in front of this guy. No telling what he'll try. My only option is to push forward and avoid him if he tries to collide with me. I'm one of the best drivers I know, so I know I won't have a problem keeping us safe. It's a matter of what this fucker is going to do.

"I need both hands, honey. Otherwise, I'd be hugging you and holding your hand. But I need to get us the fuck out of here, okay?"

I see her nod out of the corner of my eye. She already has her seatbelt on, thankfully, because her hands are shaking as much as her body is. I'm surprised she got it on by herself. I keep my eyes on the headlights in front of me. I've decided I'm not making a move until he does. If he comes straight, I'm going straight. If he turns around, I'm waiting until I can't see his taillights before I turn around. Either way, I'm making my move quickly.

Emma is taking deep breaths and holding onto her seatbelt like it's the only thing keeping her alive. The second those headlights move, she's plastered against the seat and making small, fearful whimpering noises that send my protective instincts into overdrive.

"I got you, Em. I'm not letting anything happen to you. I promise."

"Yes, sir."

Those words tighten my chest. They're a turn on, but right now, it's like she just stabbed my heart. I can hear how much trust she's putting in me to protect her. I don't think she realizes I'd lay my life down if it meant saving hers.

The headlights cut across the road, and I force myself to breathe out. They slice through the woods before disappearing and being replaced with taillights. I stay right where I am until the taillights are gone. I see no headlights coming at me.

I quickly turn around, leaving him no time to come at us with his lights off and t-bone us. Fuck that. With Emma still gripping her seatbelt, I take off down the road, my eyes roaming all over the place. I keep checking my mirrors. Once I come to the stop sign, I look in all directions and roll right through it. I want to get her back to the relative safety of the B&B. Somewhere I have control.

When I reach the parking lot, I quickly find a spot. "Don't get out, Em. Let me get around to your side and get you out. I need to check around."

"Yes, sir," she whispers, her voice defeated. I hate that sound. I hate every part of it. I don't like her being scared. I definitely don't like when she feels defeated.

I quickly move to her side of the car after I park and get out. I'm on high alert. I'm always carrying a weapon with me. Tonight is no different. I'm fully prepared to use it if I have to.

I open her door. She looks up at me, waiting for my command. I hold out my hand for her and help her out. Shielding her with my body, she takes the bags from the floor of the car. I'm shocked she still has everything. I'll have to ask her why she didn't drop everything when she started running.

I place my hand on her lower back, being very mindful that she's not exposed to any threat as I rush her inside.

"Oh my!" Mrs. Danvers says, putting a hand to her heart. "You found her! Thank heavens!" She rushes to us both the second the door closes and hugs us both. For a woman her age, she definitely has some strength.

"I found her," I say, hugging them both.

Emma keeps her grip on me tight, and my heart shatters at how scared she is. I want to lecture her about going off like that on her own, but I know she's already beating herself up about it. I don't need to add to that.

My job is to get her out of her head.

"I'm so relieved to see you back, ma'am," Mr. Danvers says. He joins in the hug, and when he lets go moments later, I take Emma's hand and lead her upstairs to our room.

I close the door and put my head against it after I get us into the room. I kick off my boots. "Em, what the fuck were you thinking?" I ask. I can't stop the words. I want to comfort her, but I need to know what was going through her head.

"I wasn't," she whispers.

I turn towards her. Her head is down. Her hands are folded in front of her. She looks completely dejected.

And she's shivering.

The dominant in me takes complete control. I need to take care of her above all else. I walk towards her. She doesn't move. I unzip her coat and take it off. She's truly soaked. The coat is waterproof, thankfully, so the top part of her is dry, but I can't say the same for the lower half. No wonder she's shivering.

I hang up her coat. She stays still when I go to the dresser and find a pair of my sweats and a hoodie. She didn't bring anything warm to sleep in or lounge in because she's used to being under covers and warm. And if she gets cold, I'm usually always there to cuddle with her.

I put the sweats and sweatshirt on the bed on my way back to her. I hear her sniffle as I kneel down to help with her boots. "Are you crying? Or are you getting sick?" I focus on unlacing her boots. She doesn't answer. I look up when she puts one hand on my shoulder to steady herself while I pull off her boots. She's wiping her eyes.

"I'm sorry, Jake," she whispers. "I shouldn't have left." Her teeth chatter as she shivers.

I toss her boots towards the door as I stand. "I just need to get you warm. We can talk after that."

Emma takes a breath and grips the fabric of my thick coat. She pulls me close to her. Roughly. I'm confused… until her lips crash against mine. Like a tidal wave, every single lustful thought and feeling of love I have for this girl rushes to the surface. I wouldn't be able to hold back even if I tried.

I thrust my tongue into her mouth as I grip the nape of her neck so I can deepen the kiss. She yanks the zipper of my coat down and practically rips it off. I don't know what's happening, but there's nothing in this world that's getting me to stop her. I promised myself I'd tell her I want a relationship but on her terms, but I completely forget.

Suddenly, with our lips locked together, it becomes a frenzied, chaotic mess of clothes flying every which way as we make our way to the bed. Emma can't seem to get close enough to me. I can't get close enough to her either. I need to be inside her.

Now.

Chapter Five

❄ Emma ❄

The backs of my knees hit the bed. Jake pushes me down so I'm sitting on it as he kneels. He pulls my pants off with my underwear, peeling the wet, heavy material off my legs. I'm both cold and hot all at the same time.

He tosses them aside before quickly standing and pinning me to the bed with his body. He kisses me deeply with a low groan. I wrap my legs around his waist, pulling him closer. I need to feel him. All of him. His pants are still on. There's too much between us. I need them off.

"Jake… please…," I whimper. The need to feel him is becoming too strong to bear.

His lips crash to mine again in a feral and dominating kiss. "Not yet. Way too many things I want to do to you. The first? To spank your ass red while making you tremble for my tongue."

My eyes widen. I wet my suddenly dry lips with my tongue. I feel my pussy getting wetter. He grins before pinning my wrists with one hand and fucking my mouth with his tongue. His body moves against me. I wrap my legs even tighter around his waist and grind into him, needing more friction. The seam where his zipper is hits the right spot just perfectly.

I let out a squeak when I'm suddenly flipped onto my front. Jake grips my hips, pressing a kiss to my butt before tugging my hips up until my knees are pressed against the bed. Without warning, his hand slaps my bottom, leaving a delicious sting in its wake. I moan and arch as I shiver. He slaps my butt again just as his tongue slides into my pussy from behind.

"Oh! Jake!" I fist the blanket under me and close my eyes as I arch even more into him.

"What are you being punished for, sexy girl?" I jerk as he blows cold air across my pussy.

"Oh! Jake!" I shudder and moan. "F-for running off."

"Good girl." He buries his tongue back into my pussy. I feel him twirl his tongue inside me just as his palm connects with my butt cheeks again. I can feel my pussy getting even wetter for him.

"Ah!" I jerk back into his tongue. My thighs tremble as my pussy pulses.

"Fuck, baby. You're dripping for me," He trails his tongue down to my clit and nips it. I moan low again "Does my girl like being spanked?"

I throw my head back as his palm comes down on my bottom again. "Ah! Yes!"

He pulls back, nipping my pussy as he palms my ass with both hands. "Your ass is such a pretty red." His palms connect with it once more. I feel my pussy become even wetter as I arch back into his hands. "You're fucking soaked, pretty girl." He rumbles.

My eyes roll back when I feel him bury his tongue back into my pussy with a sexy growl. I arch with a moan as his palm slaps my butt again. "Ah! Jake! I'm going to come…!"

"Not without permission. You don't have it." I feel Jake pull away. "You're not coming until I say. And I don't say." I glance over my shoulder, and my eyes hungrily take in every inch of skin he exposes as he slips out of his pants and boxer briefs that leave nothing about his length to the imagination.

I lick my lip as his hard dick bobs against his stomach. "Please Jake… I need you…"

"Shh, baby, I got you." He climbs back onto the bed behind me. "But you're gonna have to work for it after a stunt like that." I shiver as he leans over me, kissing my neck. I moan as he rubs the head of his dick through my wetness, brushing against my clit, teasing me. My pussy pulses in anticipation of feeling him again.

His fingers tangle in my hair, gripping lightly as he turns my head towards him. He crashes his lips to mine, sucking on my tongue hungrily with a low growl as he slams into my pussy in one swift and strong thrust.

"Oh, Jake!" I scream into the kiss as my pussy spasms uncontrollably around him. How could I have forgotten how big he is? How perfectly he fills my pussy? It's like I was made for him.

He nips my lip as he pulls back with a moan. "Baby..., you're so tight."

I moan as his hips press against my sore butt cheeks. He thrusts slowly but hard. My butt throbs in pain as his skin slaps against mine while he drills into me. It just makes my pussy even wetter, and I clamp around his thick dick. I have no control. It all belongs to him. My pussy is greedy. It needs him. I'm so close to coming. I know I'll be making a mess.

I push back into him, meeting his thrusts and enjoying walking the tight line of pain and pleasure. "Jake...," I moan. We're in a B&B. There's no way I can scream out the way I want to for him. So instead, I moan and breathe out his name.

He grips my hips tighter and growls in my ear as he pulls me back into his thrusts, causing him to slide deeper. "Tell me you're mine."

My mind tailspins. Do I want to be his? Does he mean it? Am I really his? His hand slaps my bottom again as he thrusts. Instantaneously, I'm out of my head. It's like he knew I went right to that dark place and knew exactly how to get me out of it.

I scream into the mattress and soak him even more. "I'm yours!"

"And you're never going to run off like that again." He kisses my neck after growling against it once more. My entire body trembles as the vibration of his voice when it reverberates through me.

"Oh!" My eyes fly open when Jake starts rubbing my clit. The right pressure and pace has me spiraling off an invisible cliff. "I'm gonna come, Jake!" I can't stop it. Even when Jake stops rubbing my clit and stops thrusting, the orgasm washes over me.

I scream into the bed, gripping the sheets in my fists tighter. My pussy clamps down over him and pulses erratically. My hips jerk. My thighs and legs tremble. I mumble his name over and over until my body is jello.

When I finally start coming down from the explosions in my head, I realize I made a huge mistake.

"Oh no," I whisper.

"Oh, yes," Jake rumbles. His tone has dropped several octaves and sounds so dominant that I nearly come again.

He slowly pulls out. He sounds dangerous, but when my back hits the mattress and I dare to look up at him, he looks wild. Savage, even.

I have no chance to cover my mouth before he drives into me again. My body, still not anywhere near in my control, arches off the bed. "Jake!" I howl. "Oh!"

"If you come again without me, you're gonna be in a lot of trouble," he growls.

"Yes, sir!"

"Don't scream. You're gonna get us in trouble." His smirk tells me he's enjoying me losing control, but he's right. So, as he pulls me into his thrusts while he pounds into my pussy, I submit completely to him, throwing a hand over my mouth to muffle my sounds.

He brings me closer again, but this time, he stops everything until I come down. I whimper and gasp for breath, but before I can catch it, he's pounding into me again and again and again. I get close once more, and he pulls completely out. He lays down on his side as I, once again, try and catch my breath. My mind is spinning, but for once, there's nothing in it but him. Just Jake. Here. In this moment.

Wanting me.

Needing me like I need him.

Jake grips my leg as he pulls me so my back is flush against his chest. He hooks my leg over his thighs as he drives into me again. I still gasp and moan at the size of him. He's perfect. He fills me just right.

Keeping the position, the arm that's underneath me wraps around my chest. He uses his forearm to rub against my nipples. His other hand moves slowly up my body until it reaches my neck. He gently grips it until he hears me let out a moan.

Only then does he start thrusting. Slowly. Teasingly. "I can't believe you came before my command. Such a bad girl," he rumbles against my neck before kissing it. His thrusts get faster, harder, and deeper. "What should I do about that, naughty girl?"

I pant at all of the sensations he's causing to erupt throughout my body. I turn my face into the pillow because I want to scream, but I'm met with his upper, very muscular, arm. I bite into it, not hard, as our skin slaps together. I sound so wet right now. Knowing he's the reason why makes me want to come again for him.

I don't dare.

"I… don't… Jake…" Nothing that comes out of my mouth makes sense.

"I'm gonna come so deep inside you that you're going to leak my come for days," he growls. "You're gonna know who you belong to." He grunts as he thrusts hard, nearly launching me off the bed. Thankfully, he's holding me close. "You're gonna know not to run from me. And you're damn sure not ever going to come without my command first again."

"Yes, sir!" I scream into his arm. The only coherent sentence to come from my lips. My pussy is dripping. It's pulsing erratically, and I know I'm gonna come, but I have to hold back. If I don't, I know he's going to torture me in the most delicious of ways. The end result would be me not getting to orgasm.

I don't want that.

I need to come.

Jake pushes against me, burying himself in me and me against the bed. With a low and possessive roar against my neck, he fulfills every single promise he just made. He comes so deeply inside me that I'll be feeling him for days.

"Who do you belong to, baby?" He kisses across my back to my shoulders. His dick doesn't move but the fact that it's pulsing inside me makes my eyes roll back.

"Yours," I whisper. "I'm all yours. Forever."

"Good girl."

Once he finishes, I expect him to do something to finish me off, but he doesn't. I know instinctively that's my punishment. Instead, he leaves his tip inside me. We're both a mess, but I don't want to clean up. Not yet. I want to feel him just a little while longer.

"Oh, Jake…," I whisper when I finally manage a normal breath.

Jake wraps me up tighter. "I'm not letting you come, little hellion." He pulls the blankets over us. "That's your punishment. Don't ever think of running off on me like that again. Even if it's handcuffed, I'm leaving here with you."

I close my eyes, exhausted and content, even without the release. I nod into his arm and let him hug me as I slowly drift off to sleep.

Chapter Six

❄ Jake ❄

(Valentine's Day)

When I wake up, it's still dark outside. Emma is sleeping peacefully in my arms. My dick is still just at her entrance, though it somehow slid out during the night. I grumble a little bit about that, but not too much because I'm hard as steel once more. All it took was the feel of her skin against my length.

After she fell asleep, I carefully got out of bed and went to the bathroom. I got a washcloth and cleaned myself up. Then I grabbed one for her. While she was sleeping, I cleaned her up. It was both a huge turn on and one of the most upsetting things I've had to do. I love how beautiful she looks covered in my come.

I reach down and start stroking myself. Slowly. I want to admire every inch of her and take my time doing it. Her neck is elongated, perfect to kiss. Her perky tits are arched for me. It takes all of my willpower not to circle her nipples with my tongue as I let my fingertips trail down her sexy tummy to the apex between her legs.

I lick my lips when my eyes get there. The way she's laying… It would be so easy for me to push her down just a little bit to give me better access to her pussy. I can see it's wet for me. Gleaming. I wonder what kind of dreams she's having. Are they sexy? Is she dreaming of me?

Gently, I push her hip enough so she's lying almost fully on her back instead of her side. Without me having to, she spreads her legs a little more for me, and I have to look up to make sure she's still asleep. She has a half smile on her beautiful face, but she's definitely asleep. Her breathing is so peaceful and steady.

To test her, though, I lean down and lick her pussy lips slowly. She lets out the sexiest moan. Her hips jerk a little, but she doesn't wake up. Her eyes are darting around behind her eyelids, and I grin. She's deep asleep. Deep enough that I can have my fun and make her feel good at the same time.

I use my thumbs to spread her vertical lips apart before I slide my tongue from her pussy hole up to her clit again and again. She responds to me like a good girl, but stays in her deep sleep. I hope I'm influencing her dream.

Every arch, jerk, tremble, and shiver she gives me makes my dick harder. I turn my head so I can thrust my tongue inside her. I moan low and deep while I rub her clit and flick it. I watch her stomach tighten as her walls start to collapse around my tongue. I fucking love the way she feels when she comes, but it's that sexy breath out as her eyes roll back that gets me.

Her release hits her, and she writhes a little bit as she moans and breathes, "Jake…"

I lick her slower and slower until she starts to come down, but I need to feel her pulsing like that around my dick as I come. I shift and slide my cock into her with a low grunt as I cage her under me. I'm praying she doesn't wake up as I start thrusting into her. I just need a couple of times before I break, and I'm so happy she gives it to me.

"Fuck, yes…" I bury my dick deep inside her and grunt when I fill her with all of me. I thrust a couple of times just to make sure my come is deep inside her. Not that I want to impregnate her. I just want her to know she's fucking mine.

❄❄❄

The sun is just coming up when I wake up again. Emma is stirring in my arms and making an adorable noise when she yawns and stretches. I smile and bury my face in her lavender scented hair. I hug her tighter and bite my cheek to keep from growling when she clenches around the tip of my dick, which is still happily seated inside her.

"Mmm…," she murmurs. A moment later, she stiffens. I can feel what's going through her mind, but we're not doing all that this time. She's not running.

"You're beautiful," I rumble against the back of her head before kissing the nape of her neck.

"Jake… we -"

"Are right where we belong," I finish for her. I'm not letting her get in her head. I don't care how much reassurance it takes.

"But -"

"No. Nothing between us is getting ruined. I'm not going to even entertain the possibility. I won't sit here and promise you that everything will be fine because that's me giving into the thoughts in your mind that say it might not be. I love you. Unconditionally. We have a very solid foundation. You and I are going to make it."

"I just -"

I shake my head and shift enough so I'm looking directly at her when I turn her head. I kiss her shoulder then her. "Stop. Stop allowing all of those intrusive thoughts to dirty up what you know is a good thing. Why do you think none of our relationships have worked out, Em? It's because it's always been us. We're endgame."

Emma looks at me with both wonder and shock in her eyes. I don't know why I'm seeing shock, though. She knows all of this. She knows I've always been good at easing her fears. I should be. I've loved her since the second I laid eyes on her. She's always been everything I've ever wanted. I have no idea why I never made a move. I should've made her mine years ago.

She finally relaxes, and I lean in and kiss her. The tension releases from her body with each swipe and flick of my tongue. She turns in my arms and pushes me on my back while she climbs on top of me. My hands automatically find her hips as my eyes roam her body.

"My fuck, baby girl. Look at you." I lick my lips as I trace all of her peaks and curves with my gaze.

She blushes and traces my abs. "Why do I feel like I just had sex with you like five minutes ago?"

I smirk and squeeze her pretty ass. "It was a couple hours ago."

The squeak that leaves her lips makes my dick twitch against my stomach. She pauses mid-trace and watches it as it grows harder and harder until it's standing straight up. Her lips part in an adorable 'O' that has me grinning like an idiot.

"Wow," she whispers. I'm pretty sure she has no idea I can hear her.

"You should do something about that," I rumble, watching her fascination.

Her eyes snap to mine. "I've never seen a guy so big. How do you even fit?"

I can't help but laugh. "Honey, we're made for each other. You think all women can take all of me like you can? Not a chance. You're his home." I wink teasingly as she giggles, and then I immediately gasp when she grasps my cock in her small hand. "Fuck." I drop my head back as she strokes it slowly.

"I should probably help him get home. He looks lost." She shifts and rubs my tip through her wetness before positioning it at her entrance.

"Troublemaker," I tease as I watch her.

"Your troublemaker?" she asks, a hopeful edge to her tone.

I reach down and help guide my length inside her as I look her directly in her eyes. "Always mine," I rumble possessively.

She breathes out a sigh as she takes me inch by inch deep into her pussy. She's my home. My literal everything. I'm nothing without her. I was an absolute idiot for allowing her to be with anyone other than me all these years.

She's stood by me through everything without question, and as I take her slowly and passionately, pouring my entire being into each thrust, I realize how badly I messed up over these years. It's something I'll kick myself for every day for the rest of my life, but I know all I can do now is show her exactly how I feel; how badly I need her, and how much I love her.

She matches my pace as she rides me. With any other girl, I'd be taking her hard and fast in this position. Hell. In any of them. I like sex, but I've never wanted to make love. I've never wanted to feel everything before. Physically, yes, but not emotionally. Not like this. This is far more different than anything I've ever felt. It's like we're sealing a connection.

It's cementing our love.

Chapter Seven

❄ Emma ❄

I walk a step behind Jake as he leads me to the breakfast room. His fingers are interlocked with mine, and I know I'm smiling from ear to ear with a deep blush because my face hurts and feels hot.

Finally.

I'm finally with the man of my dreams.

And after last night and this morning, I know it's for real. I'm not dreaming. We're really going to give this a go. He's really my boyfriend… the other half of my heart.

But what if he gets sick of you? Everything is ruined.

I shake my head slightly at myself and squeeze his hand a little harder to ground myself. Reading me like he does so well, he returns the hand squeeze, and I'm instantly comforted.

"Something smells so good," I say quietly.

Jake looks down at me when we reach the bottom of the stairs as he tugs me to his side. "I might have done something."

My stomach rumbles loudly, and I giggle. "What did you do?"

"It's a surprise." He grins as he leads me to the dining area.

The scent of something very familiar and extremely alluring almost overwhelms me. My mouth starts to water. "It smells so good. I'm starving."

"Patience, baby." He guides me to the breakfast bar where there are heated catering pans.

I look around and see people already have food on their plates. My eyes widen, and I bounce on my toes. "Biscuits and gravy? Please say biscuits and gravy! Wait. They just had that for dinner the other night." I'm still quiet so I don't disturb anyone, but the excitement I feel is evident in my tone as I look up at Jake.

He gives me a killer smile that makes my heart beat faster. "Absolutely. Nothing but the best for my girl. Anything you want."

I blush and look down at our hands clasped together. *His girl.* I barely hear anything after that. I'm really his girl. It makes me bounce on my toes even more because it's all I've wanted for so long. I've just wanted to be his, but I've settled for friends because that's what I thought he wanted.

Once we're dished up and sitting, I can't hide the smile plastered on my face. "Thank you so much for this. I don't know how you pulled this off."

He smiles as he swallows. I can't help but watch how sexy his Adam's apple looks as it bobs while his food goes down. "I asked her yesterday what she was planning for today. She asked if I had anything special I wanted. I told her that your favorite thing at any meal is biscuits and gravy. So, she agreed to make it. It was a big hit the other night."

"I really love you," I say as I shove a bite of food in my mouth. My eyes widen at what I just said. "Oh my god. I -" I cut myself and just stare at him.

He grins that wide grin again, the one I'm not sure how he manages because it has to make his face hurt. "I really love you."

My heart skips a beat and then stops entirely. I gasp and look at him in complete wonder. He really loves me back? I know he loves me. I do. But hearing the words after feeling our connection while he made the sweetest love to me this morning… I lick my suddenly dry lips. The feelings for him are so overwhelming, I could drown.

As we eat, talk comes easy. It's always been that way with us, but I'm so happy that it's like that again. No tension. Nothing standing between us. Just a brand new, happy couple who has a strong foundation of friendship to stand on.

Jake kisses my hand. "Looks like the snow has let up. I'm going to ask if it's safe to go into town. I had plans for today, but I'm not sure if I need to change them."

I nibble the inside of my cheek. "Didn't they say it's supposed to be a lot of snow? Like… a lot?"

He kisses my hands. "They did, but better to ask a local and be sure then keep checking our weather app, right?" His smile ignites my entire soul. My entire body blushes as he stands. The man is Satan's incarnate. So irresistibly sinful.

I watch him walk away and disappear into another room. Once he's out of my sight, I turn back to my food. Biscuits with sausage gravy and bacon really is my comfort food. I grew up with it and never grew out of it. No one has ever been able to get the recipe like my mom's, though. Besides me and Jake.

This one is a very, very close second.

"As long as it doesn't break during this storm. The guest room will stay yours since this storm is about to dump more snow on us. I'm glad you got here last night," Mrs. Danvers says.

"Thank you, ma'am," a deep, male voice says.

A voice that sends chills down my spine. I don't dare turn around. Instead, I finish the last bite of food as I stand up, slowly. Out of the corner of my eye, I see the man from last night near the buffet. He's kneeling and digging through a bag.

I watch in horror as he looks up at me. I don't make eye contact, but I feel like he's burning a hole in the back of my head as I walk away. I want to run, but I don't want to bring any further attention to myself. The second I'm out of sight, though, I run. I run up the stairs and to my room. I let myself in and lock the door. I deadbolt it and chain lock it from the inside then hurry to the chair that's in the corner. I curl up in it and bring my knees to my chest as I try to breathe.

Why is he here?

Why?

Why?

Did he follow me?

No, it can't be. I'm not that special. He wouldn't follow me. He had no idea where I was going. *Right?*

I nearly astral project into an entirely new universe when someone knocks on the door. I shoot a hand over my mouth and stare wide-eyed at the heavy wood. I don't dare breathe. What if it's him?

"Babe? Let me in. I left my key in there when we went downstairs."

Jake.

Oh god.

His voice propels me to move. I hurry to the door fighting back tears. "Jake?" I nearly whisper when I get there.

"It's me, baby. Flutterbies."

I hurry to unlock the door. He must hear the fear in my voice to use that word. Only Jake knows that word. It's the word he told me he'd say when he was trying to sneak into my bedroom when we were kids. My word is pookie. We only use those words with each other. We haven't used them since we were kids. Hearing it now while I'm so scared is irrationally comforting.

The second I swing open the door, I leap into his arms. He catches me, only taking a step back to steady himself.

"Fuck, baby. What happened?" Jake kicks the door closed and locks it, still holding me tightly with one hand.

"He's down there, Jake!" I cry as I shake uncontrollably and grip him as tightly as possible while burying my face in his shoulder.

"Who? Who, Em?"

"The guy from the road last night!" I shriek.

Chapter Eight

❄ Jake ❄

"What?" I nearly shout. "Where?" I let her go and turn towards the door, but Emma grabs my arm with another noise that can only be described as a terrified wolf cub. It stops me dead in my tracks.

"Don't leave me!" she manages to squeak out. Her nails dig into my arm.

"Okay. Okay, baby." I reach down just enough for my hands to grip the backs of her thighs just underneath her ass. I pick her up as she wraps herself around me as tightly as any human can. "I got you. You're okay. I got you, Em."

I adjust her so she's in my lap as I sit down on the sectional couch in the room. I push her ear against my chest as she cries so she can hear my heartbeat. I know it'll help her ground herself. Just like me hugging her and rubbing my hand up and down her back will.

After several minutes and even more deep breaths, Emma finally loosens her grip on me. She lets her arms slide down from around my shoulders, but her tiny hands still grip my shirt. I don't let her go. I'd never do that until she's ready for me to.

It takes her several more minutes to finally speak. "Why is he here?" she whispers.

"I don't know, baby. I wish I did. I can find out, but I don't want to leave you alone."

She falls quiet once more. I keep rubbing her back until I feel her take a deep breath. She starts to let go of me as she slowly sits up. I don't take my hands off her body, though.

"I think I'm okay…"

"Do you want me to go find out what's going on?"

Emma pauses and then shakes her head. "It sounded like he got stuck here after doing maintenance or something. They said they had a room for him." Her voice is low enough that I can barely make out what she's saying. "That means he's staying here…"

I nod. "Well, there's nothing we can do about that, then, but I'll protect you, baby. You know that. How about we hit that jacuzzi on the balcony? It's been calling me since I saw it. Get your mind off it and on me." I give her a winning smirk and smile even wider when she laughs.

"I didn't bring a bathing suit."

I shrug. "So? The balcony's private." I wiggle my eyebrows suggestively.

Her eyebrows shoot up. "Are you saying you want to go in that thing naked?"

"Why not? Let's go be bad."

"Oh my god."

I laugh as I pick her up while I stand. "Remember when we went skinny-dipping your freshman year?"

Emma giggles as I set her down. "Why was that a thing we did? And why was it with so many others? And why when I was a freshman?"

I laugh. "Because that's all there is to do in Cody. Get in trouble and skinny-dip." We both start taking off our clothes, not being able to take our eyes off each other. "You know, I hated every second of that?"

She raises an eyebrow. "Why?"

"It wasn't my idea. It was a buddy's idea. He wanted to see his girlfriend naked 'cuz she wouldn't give it up. I had no idea you were going to be there, but seeing the way a couple of my buddies were looking at you made me want to drown them then and there."

She nods as if something has dawned on her. "Ah… that makes so much sense now…" She grins and giggles as she takes off for the door just as I start to reach for her naked and delicious body.

I laugh and chase her. She manages to get out the door seconds before I reach her. She giggles as she gets into the jacuzzi. I follow her and sit down before pulling her into my lap.

"What makes so much sense?"

"You were always so protective of me, but that day, you wouldn't leave my side. Like you were always right there. I was super grateful because being naked in front of everyone was embarrassing, but my friends kept calling me a prude."

"I could tell you were uncomfortable. That's why I kept trying to get you to leave with me."

"I should've. Maybe you would've kissed me senseless on the way back." She giggles again. My lips crash to hers. Her arms automatically wrap around my shoulders. She moans into the kiss. Her body becomes limp in my arms as she submits to me.

Just the way I like it.

I hold her closer and deepen the kiss after tangling my fingers in her hair. My dick is already hard for her. It's pressed painfully against her thigh. I tilt her head back and kiss down her neck until my lips meet her throat. I let my teeth graze over it. She trembles for me and moans low, the vibration rumbling against my lips.

There's nothing more in the world that I want more right now than the two of us watching the snow falling while I'm pleasuring us both. I've never been more grateful for privacy walls and a black mesh weather and bug blocker. It allows us to see the scenery, but it's not easy for anyone to see onto the balcony. Not like they could anyway. We're on the second floor.

In the winter, the mesh protects from snow. In the other seasons, it protects from bugs. It's still cold, but this jacuzzi is warm and incredibly inviting.

Just like the woman in it.

I pull away from the kiss slowly and guide her to the other side of the jacuzzi so she's looking at the nature that surrounds us. She smiles at me, slightly confused, but I can feel the trust she has for me. The true belief that I'm never going to steer her wrong or hurt her.

I shift her so she's on her knees looking out at the mountains being blanketed with fresh, white, glittery snow. I slowly slide my hands over her hips to her stomach, up to her ample tits, and then to her throat. I let one hand drop down to her tits once more while the other squeezes her throat just enough to make her gasp. My lips meet the side of her neck while my other hand grips her throat. I slide into her pussy from behind as I squeeze her tits and roll her nipples between my fingers.

"Jake...," she whispers on a moan. "Oh..., Jake..." Her pussy tightens around my throbbing cock.

I groan because the way she grips me is unlike anything I've ever felt. "Baby girl, why did we wait so long?" I start thrusting deep and hard but slow. I want her to feel everything. Every inch. Every ridge. Every vein. Every throb she elicits when her muscles constrict.

"I don't know...," she whispers, shaking her head and letting it fall back on my shoulder. "I don't think it was very smart on our part."

"I should've told you the second we met that you were mine. That you'd always be mine." I hate the fact that other men have touched her before me, but I have every intention of making sure every part of her is claimed by its rightful owner.

Me.

My grip on her tightens just enough to make her arch even more into my hand and moan. I keep her back snug against my chest and thrust into her harder and harder. Water splashes up around us. The wind picks up. The snow gets heavier. Her pussy pulses uncontrollably as she meets my thrusts.

And my thrusts become more erratic. I pinch her nipples and squeeze the perfect mounds with my hand.

"I'm never gonna get enough of you," she whispers as she clenches around me.

I release her throat and use my finger and forefinger to move her face towards me so I can claim her lips. "Me either."

I plunge my tongue into her mouth at the same pace my dick is pounding into her pussy. I let the hand I had around her neck drop between her legs. I find her clit in less than a second and press my thumb against it as I rub it. The multiple sensations have her entire body quaking.

"Come for me, sexy girl. Tell the whole world you're mine," I growl. I need to hear her say those words. "Tell them you belong to me."

My stomach clenches as her pussy starts spasming. “I’m yours, Jake!” she shouts as her body jerks with her orgasm. “Jake! Jake…” She pants as she clamps down around me, coming hard. “I’m yours…, Jake…” She grips the edge of the jacuzzi as I fuck her through her orgasm.

When she finally starts coming down, I grunt and slam into her one last time. I shiver as a bolt of electricity shoots down my spine straight to my cock. I come hard. My hips slam against hers as I fill her pussy.

“Mine,” I rumble deeply and dominantly in her ear.

She leans into the edge of the jacuzzi and rests her head on her arms. I lean in and rest my head on her shoulder. I kiss along her jaw and neck soothingly. The chlorine from the water mixes with her skin and makes me wonder if chlorine actually tastes this good, or if it’s just her. I let my dick slide out of her pussy and bite my lip at her sexy as hell groan at the loss of me stretching her.

I don’t know how I managed to fight my feelings for her so long, but never again. She’s my forever.

Chapter Nine

❄ Emma ❄

"Mmm…," I murmur as my eyes flutter open.

When Jake and I came in from our jacuzzi fun, it was still light. The snow was falling really heavily. The wind was whipping it around and howling, but it was warm in the water and beautiful to watch. When we came inside, we took a shower and had another round of the most fabulous sex. Afterwards, he made a fire in the fireplace. We curled up together and watched a movie until we fell asleep.

I smile and trace his abs. He's holding me really tightly. It's dark now. The fire is just embers, and there's something on the TV that looks like an infomercial. How long did we sleep? I glance at the clock on the nightstand. It's only 4:30pm, but it looks so dark.

I blink a few times and yawn again. Movement catches my eye, and I jerk my head towards the balcony. My breath hitches in my throat. My nails dig into Jake's arm as my eyes go wide.

It can't be!

My gaze meets the cold and calculating eyes of the man from the road. *Oh my God!* I shriek in my head.

I feel my whole body start to tremble as I watch him. I want to wake up Jake, but I can hardly move. All I can do is stare as he tries to get in through the locked balcony door.

"Ow…, baby, you're gonna draw blood," Jake murmurs against my neck.

I try to let go. I just can't. Instead, I just make a noise. It sounds like a squeak. A terrified one. I can't take my eyes off the man. He's glaring at me now. "Mmm!" I squeak again, shaking more uncontrollably.

"Ow…, Em." Jake moves his other arm from around my waist and pries my fingers off his arm. "What the fuck?"

I make a mewling noise as the man glares harder before walking somewhere and disappearing. I let out a cry. "Jake!"

Jake instantly has both arms around me and has me facing him. "Hey, hey. I got you! Em, wake up, baby!"

He thinks I'm dreaming! I'm not dreaming. I'm not!

"He was here!" I scream.

"Who, Emma? Who was here?"

I point shakily to the balcony. "The man from the truck! He was here, Jake! He was out there!"

"What?" Jake looks towards the balcony suddenly on high alert. "Okay. Okay, baby. You need to let me go. I need to check." He starts getting up, but I look at him in wide-eyed shock and try grasping him again.

"Don't leave me!" I shout, panicked.

"Baby. I'm not going anywhere. You can see me the whole time. I promise. I'm not leaving you. Stay here. Let me look. I can't protect you if I don't know what I'm up against." He untangles himself from me.

"Jake!" I claw the air for him. My heart is in my mouth. I feel like I'm going to throw up and black out at the same time. "Jake!"

Jake grabs something from near the bed and hurries to the balcony. He looks out. "Son of a bitch!" He unlocks the door. I watch him as I start to hyperventilate. He rips the door open, steps out and runs to the side where I saw the man disappear.

I curl into myself and hug my knees to my chest. I want to look away and focus on breathing, but I can't. Not with Jake out there. Who knows what could happen. Maybe the man is there waiting for him. Maybe he's about to stab him or shoot him. Or grab his head and throw him off the balcony. He had to have ripped the mesh that's there to block the bugs and stuff. Right? That's the only way to get in.

Did Jake put pants on?

I see Jake lean over the balcony and hold my breath just as I hear a piercing scream. "Ah! Brady! Someone's out there trying to get in! Brady!"

My heart is beating way too fast. I'm starting to see spots.

Jake looks back at me. "Em! Do not move!"

Before I can comprehend what he's doing, Jake jumps up onto the balcony railing. Something shiny glints in his hand. I can't even scream before he's gone. I'm completely frozen in fear. I hear the woman in the room next to us scream again. Something crashes to the ground. It sounds like glass shatters.

"Stop moving!" I hear Jake yell. "Stop fucking moving! Call 911! Give me that tie!"

"Get off me!" It sounds like the man, but I don't know.

"Lock yourself in the bathroom, baby!" someone else yells.

"Emma! Lock the balcony door!" Jake yells through the walls to me.

My eyes snap to the door. It's still open, but I'm incapable of moving. Instead, I curl up in an even tighter ball and tremble. I'd be horrible in a horror movie. I wouldn't survive. I'd die because I freeze. I'd be an easy target.

Just like right now.

Anyone could kill me, and I wouldn't be able to fight.

What does this guy even want with me? Why is he after me?

My skeleton jumps out of my skin and runs away, leaving my organs and skin to scream at the knock on the door.

"Miss Marsden?" a male voice says gently. "The police are on the way, ma'am. Are you okay? It's Mr. Danvers."

The deep, male voice comforts me enough to regain some semblance of composure. I wrap the blanket around me. My mind flashes again to Jake. I didn't see him put any clothes on, and we were naked when we came inside.

"Mr. Danvers?" I say barely above a whisper once I reach the door.

"Yes, ma'am. The police are on the way. Mr. Blackwood has him subdued. I'm not sure what's going on exactly."

I peek through the peephole and see him and his wife. I unlock the door and let them in. I quickly close the door behind them. Mr. Danvers hurries to the balcony to lock the door. My heart is still beating erratically, but at least I have someone in this room that I trust.

I take a deep breath as Mr. Danvers comes back towards me and his wife. "Last night I got upset with Jake when we were in town. I decided to take our bags and walk back here. It gave me time to cool down. I forgot to turn and went the wrong way. It started to snow. I realized that I needed to turn around, so I did. This guy in a truck stopped and offered me a ride. I said no. I figured out where I was, and something about him just kind of threw me. When he turned around and followed me begging me to get in the truck, I got really scared. The snow got worse. I started running. He got out and chased me. Jake got there then. He ran from Jake."

"Oh, sweet girl." Mrs. Danvers hugs me, but I jump when the door swings open.

The first thing I see is the man in fuzzy, pink handcuffs with a tie tied around his arms. The second thing I see is my shirtless boyfriend shoving him into our room with a gun stuck in the back of his jeans. I'm too shocked to say anything or notice anything, but I'm thankful Jake put on jeans.

The man falls to the ground as Jake wraps an arm around me. "Mr. and Mrs. Danvers, I'm sorry to say your maintenance man is about to be arrested for stalking, attempted breaking and entering, and whatever else I can think of." Jake glares at the man as he pushes me behind him. "The police won't be able to get here tonight, so I'll need a place to hold him."

I look at him incredulously. "Jake?" I nearly squeak.

He looks down at me. "Not here, honey." He looks at Mr. Danvers. "Do you have anywhere we can hold him?"

Mr. Danvers shakes his head. "Nowhere that wouldn't require twenty-four-hour surveillance. Are you sure the police can't get here? They usually come in on snowmobiles if they have to."

"I didn't talk to them. The guy next door did. He said they can't get here."

"I'll call them because that doesn't sound like our guys. They go above and beyond. They'll take him out on snowmobiles. They've done it once before many years ago when we ended up with an unruly drunk." Mr. Danvers takes out a phone and turns as he calls them.

Jake wraps me in his arms as the man sits up against the wall. He's worse for the wear. His nose is bloody. His eye is swollen shut. His lip is split and bleeding. I'm pretty sure there's a cut on his head. His face looks scratched.

"What did you do to him?" I whisper to Jake.

"Nothing he didn't deserve," Jake rumbles.

"What have you done, Bobby?" Mrs. Danvers asks. "We trusted you with our home and business. How dare you repay our kindness like this?"

The man, now known as Bobby, says nothing. He just stares straight ahead like some possessed demon or something. His hands are cuffed behind his back. He poses no real danger anymore, but he sends chills down my spine. I don't want him anywhere near us or this nice couple. I don't want him near any guests. I don't want him to have the chance to hurt anyone.

"The police are coming with snowmobiles," Mr. Danvers says.

I breathe a sigh of relief and melt into Jake. He brings me to the couch and sits down with me. Mr. and Mrs. Danvers leave the room to wait for the police. I'm sure they need to feed hungry guests. I'm sorry I'll miss it, but I've lost my appetite completely.

"What the hell were you thinking?" Jake asks.

"I don't have to talk to you," Bobby growls.

"You're right. You don't. But the least you can do is tell me why the fuck you have such an obsession with my girl."

Bobby scoffs. "Right. Your girl. Some job you did of keeping track of her. She was out in the middle of a damn storm."

"Yeah? And what? You were gonna be a good boy and give her a ride here?"

"I would've taken her home and shown her what it's like with a real man. Not some little bitch like you."

I curl into Jake's side, trembling. "I don't want to hear anymore," I whisper. "Please. I understand I was lucky, and what I did was stupid."

"You would've been good, I'm sure. All nice and tight wrapped around my cock."

I whimper as Jake gets up. He punches Bobby in the face hard enough to knock him completely unconscious. I close my eyes and melt into Jake when he comes back and puts his arms back around me.

Jake kisses my head as we all fall silent. The only thing keeping me grounded is Jake's arm around me. I was so close to losing everything over my stupidity of not telling him how I felt about him a long time ago. If I'd just told him I had a thing for him way back when, this wouldn't have happened.

He's admitted that he fell for me when he first saw me, which was way before I saw him. To me, that doesn't matter. I should've said something and didn't. I let him believe I didn't like him like that. He let me believe it, too, but I still take the responsibility for it. Sometimes, guys can be dumb about those things. I should've made my feelings known.

I almost lost my life before I was able to live it.

With Jake.

Chapter Ten

❄ Jake ❄

"I'm sorry you didn't get the special Valentine's Day dinner, Em. I know you were looking forward to it," I tell Emma after we get out of the shower.

The police left with Bobby an hour ago. It turns out he had a warrant out of Texas for the murder of two women. The second Emma heard that, she burst into tears and became a sobbing mess. I sat there and held her knowing how much it killed her to hear that. Not only that two women had been killed by him, but that she was close to being his next victim. He's suspected of the disappearance of several other women, including two here in Rexford.

He was taken away in real cuffs. Not the furry ones, the couple next door gave us. Though, I wouldn't have been upset seeing the guy paraded into jail with pink, furry handcuffs.

Emma looks up at me and smiles as she shakes her head. "I'm not upset. I have you. That's all I want."

I smile, but I know my girl. She's a romantic at heart, and she loves Valentine's Day. I run my fingers through her still damp hair and grip the back of her neck. "Lucky for you, I know you better than that."

She gives me an adorably confused smile as she tilts her head. I kiss the corner of her mouth before turning and letting her go.

I make my way to a couple bags I put in the closet. One of them is a gift for her. Well, for both of us because I'm going to love taking it off her after I admire how she looks in it. The other is also a gift for her, but it's much more something just for her. It's tradition for me to get it for her every single year, and I haven't missed one yet. Even deployed, I always had a buddy deliver it for me.

I turn back to her. She's looking at me with a soft look of wonder that has me hard for her instantly. Especially since all she's wearing is a towel. Being with her in that shower couldn't come close to satiating my appetite for her. She needed me to make her feel like she was safe. I needed to feel every part of her to know she was still alive. The shower sex was hard and rough and ended way too quickly.

"Sit down, beautiful."

Emma blushes and pushes her hair behind her ear as she sits down and lets her gaze drop to her feet. I sit down next to her. "I didn't get you anything. I couldn't find anything that called to me."

I chuckle. "I have what I want, sweet girl. I have you."

Her blush deepens, and I've never been more grateful for just wearing a towel around my waist because my cock is standing straight and at attention. It doesn't take much. All she has to do is smile and I'm on my knees for her.

I hand her the first bag, and she rewards me with a sweet smile as she looks up at me. "Is that what I hope it is?"

I smirk. "You'll have to open it and find out."

She tears into the white gift bag with pink and white tissue paper. I love the way her face lights up when she sees what's in it. "A Symphony bar with toffee and almonds!"

I laugh. "Can't ever forget that." It's her favorite chocolate on the planet. I'd never dream of getting one of those heart shaped boxes with stale chocolates in it. She'd never let me live it down.

She digs down deeper, knowing full well what's in the bag. As soon as she reaches it, she smiles so brightly, it lights up the romantic setting of the lights in the room. "You didn't forget!" She pulls out a pair of fuzzy socks with hearts all over them.

"When have I ever forgotten?" I grin.

She has a collection of socks for every single holiday and wears them religiously, no matter the weather. If we're out on the Fourth of July, she'll pack the socks with her to put on after the sun goes down. I've always thought it's one of the most adorable things she's ever done.

She leans in and leaves a soft kiss on my lips. "I love you," she whispers when she pulls back. Her eyes immediately go wide when she realizes what she said, even though she's already said it. She's still not used to being able to.

I don't let her get flustered. I tangle my fingers in her hair and pull her close for another kiss. There's nothing sweet about this one. There's nothing innocent. It's a kiss that won't have a problem cementing in her mind that I feel the exact same way.

I don't let up until I feel her melt against me. Her hand, against my chest when I first pulled her close, slowly slides down my abs and rests on my hard length. It leaves no doubt what she does to me. I've been in some state of arousal ever since the moment I saw her. My first real boner happened because of her. It was embarrassing as hell trying to hide that in class. Especially with all attention on the new kid.

"I love you, Em. You've always been the calm in my chaos. You always will be. You're the other half of me. I've known it for a long time. I was just stupid. Sleeping around. Being in other relationships. Letting you be with anyone other than me. It's always been us. Always."

I pull her close again and kiss her even deeper. I feel the very second she loses herself to me. It's a feeling I've longed to feel for most of my life. Now that I know it, I'm never letting it go.

"Mmm…," Emma pulls away slowly and eyes the other bag.

I laugh and hand it to her. "Keep in mind, I bought this for you on my way out here. I know it's your size, but it's not exactly what I would've picked if I had more time to look."

She raises an eyebrow. "Should I be scared?"

I laugh again. "Maybe. But more scared of what's going to happen after."

She tilts her head and narrows her eyes. "After… what…?"

I smirk. "Open it."

She opens this one a lot more cautiously. It's a red bag with red tissue paper. I bought it hoping that we'd be here right now. I wasn't sure if she'd slam the door in my face when I showed up, but I wasn't giving up easily on her.

On us.

She pulls the gift out of the bag, and I bite my lip to keep my smirk from growing into a full blown grin. She holds up a strappy, lace, red bra and sucks her lower lip into her mouth. The bra has two straps that go down each side and attach to a matching thong. The thong has two more straps on each side that aren't attached to anything. They hang down.

"What am… I… looking at…?" Her pretty eyes are glittering when they meet mine.

"There's something else in there." I nod to the bag.

She reaches in again and pulls out red, nylon stockings. She nibbles her lip. Just that small action makes my stomach clench. I can feel the precome leaking from my tip. My hard on is becoming painful, so I squeeze it, hoping to relieve pressure. I know it's a fruitless effort, but I have to do something.

"You want me to put this on?"

"More than anything."

Emma giggles, and it's the sexiest sound I've ever heard. How did I survive this long without burying my dick in her? "Okay." She gets up and skips to the bathroom.

I lean back on the couch and put my feet up on the ottoman. I have no choice. I grip my dick and give myself a few strokes, leaving the towel in place. If I give myself skin to skin contact, it's over for me. So, I only allow slow strokes and give myself only one squeeze.

It seems like hours, but Emma finally opens the bathroom door. Her head comes out first. "I don't know if I have this on right."

"Well, come out here, baby, and let me see."

She giggles again and disappears behind the door. Moments later, she opens the door fully and shuffles out with her hands folded innocently in front of her. She's blushing so deeply, her cheeks match the lingerie. She looks down at her feet as I suck in a breath. I'm on my feet in less than a second.

"Is it right?" she asks softly when I reach her.

My hands splay over her hips and push her into a slow turn so I can take in all of her. "You're fucking perfect," I growl possessively.

No one is ever seeing her like this. The bra pushes her already perky tits up just enough to make my vision blur. The thong somehow makes her ass look tighter. My girl isn't that tall, but her legs look like they go for miles.

Once I have her facing me again, I lose the towel. In one, swift motion, I have her lifted and against the wall. She gasps when her back hits it. She automatically wraps her legs around my waist and arms around my shoulders. Her eyes are wide, but they're filled with a fire and lust I know damn well she's only shown to me. No other man in her life has ever turned her on like I have. I've always known that. I was just too stupid to act on it.

"It's always been us, Em. You make a fucking mess of me." I pull her panties aside and slam into her, thrusting hard, deep, and so fucking possessively that she's never going to doubt who she belongs to.

"Jake!" Her nails dig into my shoulders as her head falls back.

My lips latch on her throat, and I suck hard enough that I know I'll leave a mark. My mark. Right in a place no one will miss. Everyone will know this girl is all mine.

I leave bite marks across her collarbone to her shoulder as she moans and writhes for me. Each thrust makes her wetter and wetter until her pussy is erratically pulsing for me and dripping down my cock and balls, claiming me as I am her. She scratches her nails across my back as we both pant for each other.

"So fucking tight. Just for me."

"Only for you," Emma pants. Her lips hit my neck, and I feel her suck on my skin, leaving her own mark.

"Oh my fuck, baby. Come for me. Now." I pin her to the wall and reach around to rub her clit as she clamps around me.

She sucks harder on my neck as she loses complete control. Her hips jerk against mine as I slam into her and come harder than I've ever come in my life. Something about her marking me like that… I couldn't hold back even if I'd tried. I pound my come deep into her pussy as we both orgasm together. She screams into my neck, and it makes the new mark all the hotter. Especially since she doesn't move her mouth.

It takes us several moments of moans and heavy breathing before we're able to make any kind of motion whatsoever. Emma trembles, and I can tell she's nowhere near steady enough to stand on her feet, so I carry her to the bed. I kiss her softly before heading to the bathroom and starting the water in the jacuzzi tub. I add bubbles because I know she loves them.

Once I finish, I walk back out to the bed. Emma watches me with a soft, satiated look across her sweet face, and I decide in that moment, it's my favorite expression she's ever given me. Slowly, and with the utmost care, I start removing the lingerie. Emma lets me, watching my every move and mewling softly when my lips hit her skin in a soft kiss.

After getting the sexy fabric off her, I lift her in my arms and carry her to the tub. Not letting her go, I settle us both in the water, her on my lap. Her head falls against my shoulder. I start rubbing muscles I know are sore as I kiss her softly.

This.

This is what I've been missing all my life.

I don't need to chase my demons or run from them. I don't need to wonder if anyone is out there thinking about me being the one that got away because I wasn't in their bed when they woke up the next morning.

I have everything right here in my arms.

She's my best friend.

My everything.

The End

Snowed In Trilogy

Available Now

Snowed In For Christmas
Snowed In With The Stalker
Snowed In With My Best Friend

Other Books By Melony Ann

The Beautiful Dream Series

Available Now

Loving You
My Love, My Heart
Softening Lyric
Undercover Temptations
Captain Charming
Breaking Boundaries
Crashing Into You
Tactical Inferno
Ravishing Our Queen
Cherished By The Texan
Unveiling Our Passions

Box Sets Available

The Beautiful Dream Series: Box Set: Part 1
The Beautiful Dream Series: Box Set: Part 2

The Crane Family Series

Available Now

The Reluctant Mafia King
Sweet Lies
Billion Dollar Love Story
Be Mine
Protecting Her
Dangerously Forbidden Love
His Heart
Love In The Dark

Box Sets Available

The Crane Family Series

The Deimos Trilogy

Available Now

Connor's Legacy
Aryan's Alpha
Kade's Redemption

Box Sets Available

The Deimos Trilogy

The Forbidden Temptation Series

Available Now

The Detective's Forbidden Temptation
The Running Back's Forbidden Temptation
The Prez's Forbidden Temptation
The Coach's Forbidden Temptation
The Tight End's Forbidden Temptation

The Lucinio Family Series

Available Now

Rising From The Ashes
The Player's Rebel
Encrypting My Heart
Fighting My Fate
Phoenix Rising
Defending Her Honor

Multi Author Series
Piper Falls: Firehouse 49

Available Now

Ignite My Fire by Melony Ann
Regain My Fire by Kindra White
Playing With My Fire by D.L. Howe
Fight My Fire by Darley Collins
Against My Fire by Anneke Boshoff
Relight My Fire by Louise Murchie
Harness My Fire by Ayana Lisbet
Quench My Fire by Havana Wilder

Piper Falls: Station 28 Series

Available Now

Embracing My Duty by Melony Ann
Torn By My Duty by Kayla Baker
Against My Duty by Anneke Boshoff
Defying My Duty by D.L. Howe
Leave Of My Duty by Nikki A. Lamers
Fulfilling My Duty by Havana Wilder
Following My Duty by Louise Murchie
Replete In My Duty by Stacy Kristen
Accepting My Duty by Darley Collins

Let's Be Friends

Follow me on

Bookbub

Facebook

Goodreads

Instagram

Tik Tok

Visit my website
www.melonyannauthor.com

Subscribe to my newsletter and get a FREE never-seen-before NOVELLA just for subscribers!
https://www.melonyannauthor.com/exclusive-content

Join my Facebook Reader Group!
Melony Ann's Sizzling Book Nook

The official Snowed In Trilogy Playlist on Spotify
https://open.spotify.com/playlist/70PhgDd9j91K3Hb1YT6bWF?si=ZQu24OJETOS3V2etuzl0cQ

Acknowledgements

To my loves.

To my friends.

To my team.

To the Bookstagram Community.

To my family.

To all of those who believe in me and support me.

To all of those who don't.

Cover by: Carter Cover Designs

About Melony Ann

Melony Ann began writing short stories and poetry as a child. She continued honing her craft over the years until she took the plunge and began publishing her work, despite having severe anxiety.

Melony is an award winning author, winning a coveted Firebird Award, and writes contemporary romance stories that are full of suspense and a lot of steam.

When she isn't writing, she is loving her family and working to make her life something she deserves.

Melony believes that if her writing can inspire just one person, then all of her hard work is worth it.

Her hope is that her writing allows each and every one of her readers to escape for a little while. To dive into a different world one book at a time.

www.ingramcontent.com/pod-product-compliance
Lightning Source LLC
Chambersburg PA
CBHW072234190626
46809CB00017B/1925
* 9 7 8 1 9 6 1 9 6 6 7 7 2 *